THE QUEST OF EWILAN

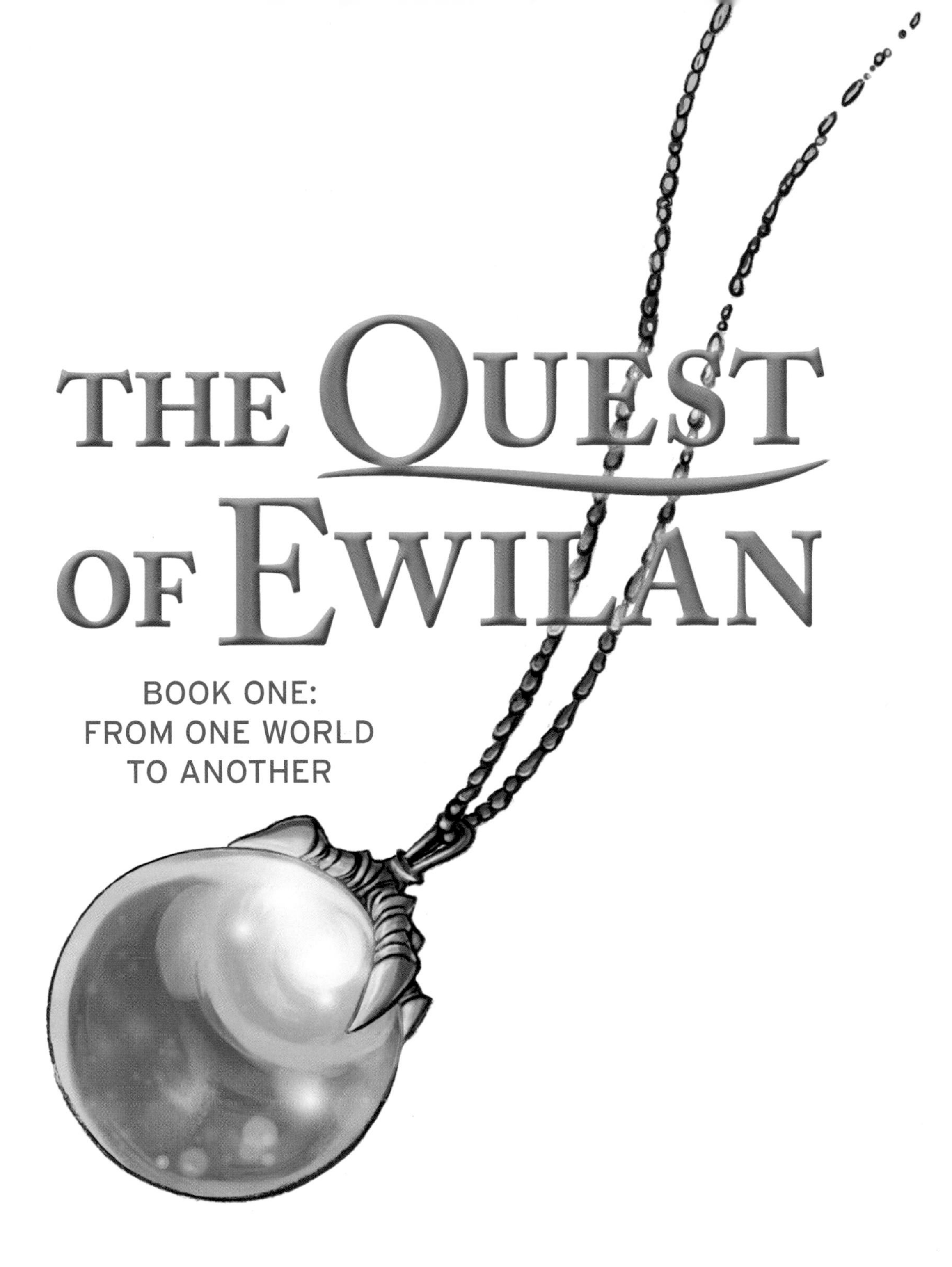

BOOK ONE:
FROM ONE WORLD
TO ANOTHER

Based on the novel by Pierre BOTTERO

Adaptation: LYLIAN
Art: Laurence BALDETTI
Coloring: Loïc CHEVALLIER

An imprint of IDW PUBLISHING

Edited by Dean Mullaney
Art Director Lorraine Turner
Translation Edward Gauvin

EuroComics.us

EuroComics is an imprint of
IDW Publishing
a Division of Idea and Design Works, LLC
2765 Truxtun Road • San Diego, CA 92106
www.idwpublishing.com

Distributed to the book trade by Penguin Random House
Distributed to the comic book trade by Diamond Book Distributors

ISBN: 978-1-68405-325-4
First Printing, August 2018

THANKS TO:
Ivanka Hahnenberger, Justin Eisinger, and Alonzo Simon.

THAT DAY, CAMILLE WAS SKIPPING SCHOOL.
SHE OFTEN SPENT LUNCHTIME IN THE QUIET OF THE LIBRARY, RATHER THAN WITH OTHER STUDENTS AT THE MIDDLE SCHOOL WHERE SHE BOARDED DURING THE WEEK.
CAMILLE LOVED THE SILENT COMPANY OF COUNTLESS BOOKS. IT GAVE HER A SENSE OF PEACE AND SERENITY, A SENSE OF WELL-BEING THAT LASTED FOR HOURS AFTERWARD.

CAMILLE WAS 4,900 DAYS OLD, OR JUST OVER THIRTEEN YEARS.
SHE WAS LOST IN THOUGHT WHEN FATE UNEXPECTEDLY CAME CRASHING IN.
BOULANGERIE
WHAT TH--?!
HEY, KID! WHAT ARE YOU, CRAZY?!
VROOOOOOOOOOOOOO
RIIII !!!

?
BOLETUS EDULIS.
?
FRRRRRRRRR
FESTERING PUSS-RIDEN SON OF A SWINE!

AH! DO PARDON MY LANGUAGE, MILADY. THE THRILL OF THE MÊLÉE DOTH MAKE ME NEGLECT MY GOOD MANNERS.
I MUST ADMIT, THESE TS'LIKS -- ALBEIT CUNNING AND LOATHSOME -- ARE WORTHY ADVERSARIES INDEED!
FEAR NOT! THE SITUATION IS WELL IN HAND!
TSSSSCHHHH....

HAH!!
TSSARRGGGH

?
TSSSSS !!
SO THERE YOU ARE, EWILAN!
LONG HAVE MY BRETHREN AND I SOUGHT YOU, THAT WE MIGHT FINISH WHAT WAS BEGUN. BUT YOU WERE NOWHERE TO BE FOUND.
AND NOW TODAY, AS LUCK WOULD HAVE IT --
-- YOU DIE!
LOOK OUT!

?
WATCH WHERE YOU'RE WALKING, YOUNG LADY!
SHE JUST RAN RIGHT OUT IN FRONT OF ME, I SWEAR!
YOU MUST HAVE BEEN GOING TOO FAST, BUDDY!
THERE WASN'T ANY TIME TO STOP!
AND THEN SHE JUST VANISHED!
HAS ANYONE CALLED THE POLICE?
POOR GIRL! SHE MUST BE CAUGHT UNDERNEATH SOME-WHERE!
CAMILLE THOUGHT SHE WAS MERELY DREAMING AGAIN. IT HAD BEEN HAPPENING A LOT LATELY.
SOME FARAWAY FOREST, A LOSER OF A KNIGHT, AND SOME INSECTOID MONSTER!
SHE OFTEN LET HER MIND WANDER DOWN THE WINDING BYWAYS OF HER IMAGINATION.
OKAY, CAMILLE, TIME TO SNAP OUT OF IT!
TO STRANGE PLACES, OTHER WORLDS, WITH PEOPLE AND EVENTS THAT SEEMED VERY REAL TO HER.
SUCH IMAGES WOULD ALWAYS FADE AWAY WHENEVER CAMILLE CAME TO HER SENSES. ALWAYS, THAT IS...
...UNTIL TODAY!

HEY, CAMILLE!
YOU DEAF?
?
MISSED YOU IN CLASS TODAY. FORGET TO SET YOUR ALARM?
SALIM!
pretty poodle
toilettage
WHAT'S THE MATTER, GIRL!
TROUBLE WITH YOUR PARENTS AGAIN?
SALIM...
...I THINK I JUST VISITED A PARALLEL DIMENSION!
HAHAHA
I'M TOTALLY SERIOUS! I REALLY DID TRAVEL TO ANOTHER WORLD!
toilettage
AWESOME! MY BROTHER DOES THAT ALL THE TIME WHEN HE HAS TO GET AWAY FROM MARTIANS!
HAHAHAHA !
DON'T BE A JERK, SALIM. YOU DON'T EVEN HAVE A BROTHER.
THIS REALLY HAPPENED, I'M TELLING YOU!
RELAX, GIRL. I BELIEVE YOU. BESIDES, IT'S LIKE NOT LIKE YOU LIVE IN THE SAME WORLD AS EVERYBODY ELSE ANYWAY.

ALICE IN WONDERLAND
CUT IT OUT, SALIM!
OKAY, FINE. BUT FIRST, HOW MUCH IS 357 X 629?
224,553... WHY?
NO REASON. AND WHAT'S THE CAPITAL OF BURKINA FASO?
OUAGADOUGOU. WHAT ARE YOU TRYING TO PROVE, SALIM?
HUMOR ME.
WHO INVENTED THE TELEPHONE?
ALEXANDER BELL, 1876.
ICE CREAM
THE EARLY VERSION WAS A TRANSMITTER ATTACHED TO A BATTERY-POWERED ELEC--
OKAY, STOP! JUST CHECKING TO SEE IF YOU WERE STILL SANE.
DON'T WORRY, SALIM, I'M FINE. NOW THAT I'VE REASSURED YOU, HOW 'BOUT SOME ICE CREAM?
GIRL, THAT'S THE BEST IDEA YOU'VE HAD SO FAR...TWO DOUBLE SCOOPS FOR ME AND MY PAL!

SO YOU'RE NOT AFRAID YOUR PARENTS WILL FIND OUT YOU SKIPPED CLASS?
FIRST OF ALL, MAY I REMIND YOU: THEY'RE NOT MY PARENTS.
AND HONESTLY, AS LONG AS I GET GOOD GRADES AND BEHAVE...
...THEY DON'T GIVE A DAMN WHAT I DO.
WHOA! TA-DAA!
DID YOU SEE THAT? SO TELL ME...HOW DO YOU KNOW THIS PARALLEL UNIVERSE OF YOURS IS REAL?
BECAUSE THIS TIME I BROUGHT SOMETHING BACK!
THAT THING LOOKS AWESOME. CAN I HOLD IT?
BE MY GUEST.
I-I CAN'T!
WHAT DO YOU MEAN, YOU CAN'T?
IT-IT'S LIKE WHEN I TRY TO GRAB IT, MY FINGERS ARE REPELLED!
HEY, RASTA BOY!
?!

UNDER THAT HAIR, I CAN'T TELL IF YOU'RE A BOY OR A GIRL !
HEH HEH HEH...
C'MON, CAMILLE, LET'S GO.
BUT...
WHERE DO YOU THINK YOU'RE GOING, RASTA BOY? AFRAID WE'LL STEAL YOUR GIRL?
BUNCH OF BRAIN-DEAD JERK-WADS!
WE SHOULD STAND UP TO THEM!
NO, 'CAUSE...ONE, THAT'S WHAT THEY WANT. TWO, THEY'RE BIGGER THAN US AND THERE ARE MORE OF THEM ...AND THREE, BECAUSE I'M USED TO IT.
HAHAHAHAHAHA

?
SO THERE'S JUSTICE AFTER ALL! CHECK OUT THAT SORRY BUNCH OF LOSERS!
THEY LOOK LIKE THEY JUST FELL OUT OF THE WRONG END OF A COW!
C'MON, SALIM, LET'S GO. THEY'RE NOT GOING TO KEEP ROLL-ING AROUND ON THE GROUND ALL DAY JUST FOR YOUR AMUSEMENT.
ANYWAY, IT'S SIX ALREADY! GOTTA GO--I'M RUNNING LATE.
OKAY, GIRL. BUT WATCH OUT FOR THOSE PARALLEL UNIVERSES, GOT IT?
THOSE BULLIES...
THAT BENCH...
BBZZZ
EASY THERE, CAMILLE. IT'S NOT LIKE YOU'RE A WITCH, AND TELEKINESIS ISN'T EXACTLY REAL.
KEEP YOUR FEET ON THE GROUND...

?
WELL, CAMILLE. YOU SEEM TO HAVE A REAL PROBLEM WITH PUNCTUALITY.
I REALIZE THAT TEENAGED GIRLS ARE ALWAYS RUNNING TEN MINUTES BEHIND. I'LL GIVE YOU THAT, BUT EVEN SO -- AN ENTIRE HALF HOUR?
EXPLANATIONS?
NO, MA'AM. I'M SORRY.
IN THAT CASE, NO SOCIAL MEDIA FOR YOU THIS WEEK.
DINNER'S AT 7:30. IN THE MEANTIME, YOU WILL WAIT IN YOUR ROOM SO YOU WON'T BE LATE.
DON'T YOU WANT TO HEAR HOW MY DAY WENT?
WHAT IF I SAID I SKIPPED SCHOOL TODAY?
WE'D BE VERY DISAP-POINTED IN YOU, CAMILLE.
WE'VE GIVEN YOU A GREAT DEAL. DO TRY AND BE ATTENTIVE TO YOUR OBLIGATIONS.
BUT SURELY THAT WAS A JEST.
RIGHT. A CLUMSY ONE, TOO, I'M AFRAID.
I FORGIVE YOU.
BE A GOOD GIRL AND GO TO

PAINTERS' TOWERS. SALIM'S APARTMENT.
PYTHAGORAS, OL' PAL, LET'S MAKE IT WORK OUT THIS TIME.
AAAAND... NOPE. STILL NOPE. PFFF...
SALIM! WE'RE GOING TO BED. G'NIGHT!
WHY DIDN'T YOU COME PLAY WITH US?
NEED HELP WITH YOUR HOMEWORK?
SURE DO, GIRLS! NOW, GOOD NIGHT AND CLOSE THAT DARNED DOOR.
CAN'T I GET FIVE MINUTES OF PEACE IN THIS HOUSE?
HE'S SUCH A PARTY-POOPER!
HMPH. AS IF! I WISH CAMILLE WAS HERE...
THE GOLDEN MEAN ARISTOTLE

KKRRRRRRRR
?
KSH-KLANG!
CRASHHH!
WOOF!
WOOF!
GRRRR
OOOOWEEEOOOOWEEE
OOOWEEEEOOOOOWEEEEEE!
OOOWEEEEOOOOWEEE
GRRR!
WOOF!
WOOF!
OOOWEEEEOOOOWEEEEE

OOOWEEEEOOOOOWEEEEEEEOOOWEEEEOOOOOWEEEEEE!
RRRRR
WOOF!
WOOF!
GRRR!
MAXIM! WHAT'S GOING ON?
NOT THE FOGGIEST, MY DEAR. I'LL LOOK INTO IT!
CAMILLE !
ARE YOU HURT ?
HEAVENS, CAMILLE! WHAT HAVE YOU DONE NOW?

THE NEXT DAY
CHESTNUT MIDDLE SCHOOL.
...SO NOT ONLY DID I GET FREAKED OUT, I GOT CHEWED OUT, TOO!
YOUR DAD DIDN'T BELIEVE YOU EITHER?
NOT AT ALL! WHEN HE SAW THE HEDGES WERE ALL TRAMPLED AND THAT GENGHIS, ONE OF THE DOGS, WAS WOUNDED, HE FIGURED IT WAS A PROWLER.
BUT MY MOTHER WAS CONVINCED I'D BROKEN THE WINDOW AND SET OFF THE ALARM!
THEY CALL THE COPS?
YEAH, BUT NO ONE BOTHERED COMING OUT. JUST TOOK A COMPLAINT OVER THE PHONE.
JEEZ, THAT SUCKS! WHAT'LL YOU DO NOW?
NO IDEA. BUT THANKS FOR LISTENING. BETWEEN THAT SPIDER AND THE WHOLE WORLD-HOPPING THING, I FEEL LIKE I'M GOING NUTS.
ANY TIME, GIRL. DON'T YOU WORRY --
RRIIINNG
-- SALIM, THE LION OF CAMEROON AND HIS LEGENDARY DEXTERITY ARE HERE TO SAVE YOU FROM ALL DANGER!
FRANÇAIS
LION OF CAMEROON, HUH?
WHAT? DON'T

"WITH HIS HEAD, HE SAYS NO...WITH HIS HEART, HE SAYS YES.
"WHAT HE'S TAUGHT HE REFUSES...WHAT HE LOVES, HE ACCEPTS.
"ON HIS FEET, HE IS QUIZZED, ALL THE PROBLEMS PUT TO HIM... HE ERASES THEM ALL, MAD LAUGHTER RUNS THROUGH HIM.
"THE WORDS AND THE NUMBERS, THE DATES AND THE NAMES...THE SENTENCES AND TRICK QUESTIONS.
"AND DESPITE THREATS..."
AND DESPITE THREATS FROM THE TEACHER, 'NEATH JEERS FROM THE GIFTED...IN EVERY COLOR OF THE RAINBOW...
ON THE BLACKBOARD OF SORROW...
...HE DRAWS THE FACE OF HAPPINESS.
TA-DAA.
OOOH !
NICE !
LOOK !
?!
?
HA HA HA !!

CAMILLE AND SALIM MANAGED TO MAKE IT THROUGH THE REST OF THE DAY WITHOUT FURTHER INCIDENT.
YOU SURE THAT WAS YOU?
TOTALLY!
IT WAS THE SAME FEELING AS YES-TERDAY, IN THE PARK. I PICTURED WHAT I WANTED -- OR RATHER, I ALTERED REALITY IN MY HEAD.
WELL, WE ALL DO THAT.
NO. THIS WAS DIFFERENT...AND I COULD FEEL IT.
IF I IMAGINE SOME-THING, I CAN SEE IT SHARP AND CLEAR AS SOME-THING REAL.
AND THAT'S NOT ALL! I CAN ALTER IT AT WILL: TOUCH UP A LINE, DARKEN A COLOR, FUDGE A DETAIL...LIKE IN A DRAWING!
WHAT AM I GOING TO DO?
EASY. IF THIS WERE A MOVIE, YOU'D LEARN TO HARNESS YOUR POWERS AND USE THEM TO DUKE IT OUT WITH THAT SPACE SPIDER!
THIS ISN'T A MOVIE, SALIM. I'M IN DEEP TROUBLE -- UP TO MY NECK!
WASN'T THAT YOUR WAY HOME?
NUH-UH! WITH BIG SPIDERS AROUND, I'M WALKING YOU HOME TONIGHT!
NO OFFENSE, SALIM, BUT IT WAS ALMOST THREE FEET TALL AND HELD OFF TWO DOGS THAT COULD POLISH US BOTH OFF AND STILL BE HUNGRY FOR MORE.
DON'T YOU WORRY! BACK IN CAMEROON, WE EAT SPIDERS -- THE BIGGER, THE TASTIER!
GREAT, SALIM. HOW VERY REASSURING.

WOW, CAMILLE, I ALWAYS FORGET YOU LIVE IN SUCH A POSH NEIGHBORHOOD. EVER FEEL LIKE THE FRENCH PRINCESS OF BEL-AIR?
HA, HA, SALIM! VERY FUNNY!
THANKS FOR WALKING ME HOME. SEE YOU TOMORROW.
ANYTIME. SEE YA!
AAAH!!
CAMILLE!
HOLD ON! I'M COMING!
?!

SCRAM, YA DAMN BUGS!
SO...WHICH ONE SHOULD I EAT FIRST?
WHERE ARE THOSE DUMB DOGS OF YOURS?
BELIEVE...LOCKED UP BY DAY?
KKRRRRRR
SALIM!

IT'S OKAY, SALIM. YOU CAN OPEN YOUR EYES NOW.
UH...WHERE ARE WE?!
IN A PARALLEL WORLD. AND JUST IN TIME, TOO. AGAIN!
BUT -- HOW'D YOU DO THAT, CAMILLE?
NO CLUE. JUST LIKE I HAVE NO CLUE WHERE WE ARE.
I'VE ONLY BEEN HERE ONCE. LONG ENOUGH TO SEE A KNIGHT GO FLYING THROUGH THE AIR AND NARROWLY AVOID GETTING HACKED TO BITS BY SOME GIANT LIZARD.
YOU NEVER SAID ANYTHING ABOUT GIANT LIZARDS!
OH, GREAT. THEY FOLLOWED US!
KKKSSSSSSSSS

CAMILLE --
STAY CALM, SALIM. THIS TIME, WE'RE GOING TO HAVE TO FIGHT.
FWOOOSHH
?!
YAAAAAH!!!!

GET READY FOR A TASTE OF THE LION OF CAMEROON, SUCKERFACE!
SHHHHHH
SHLAKK
!!
PARDON ME. MY FIRST ARROW SEVERED THIS IN FLIGHT.

I SHOULD BE CURIOUS TO LEARN THE REASON FOR YOUR PRESENCE HERE, AND WHAT YOUNGSTERS LIKE YOURSELVES HAVE TO DO WITH THE **WALKERS**.
BUT FIRST, WE MUST LEAVE THIS PLACE.
THE CORPSES OF THESE CREATURES WILL DRAW EVERY CARRION FEEDER NEARBY.
MY NAME IS **EDWIN**.
FOLLOW ME.
CAN YOU GET US HOME?
I DON'T KNOW HOW. SORRY, SALIM.
THEN I GUESS WE'D BETTER DO LIKE THE MAN SAYS.
THESE WOODS ARE PRETTY, BUT I'M NOT SURE I LIKE THE CRITTERS THAT LIVE HERE.
HEY! MR. EDWIN! WAIT UP!

GOT ANY MATCHES?
NOPE. NO LIGHTER, EITHER.
WE'VE BEEN WALKING FOR AN HOUR IN TOTAL SILENCE.
HE'S OFFERED NO EXPLANATIONS, AND THEN HE TELLS US TO LIGHT A FIRE? OUR KINDLY RESCUER IS REALLY GETTING ON MY NERVES!
WHOA THERE, GIRL. LIGHTING A FIRE WITH NO MATCHES IS NOTHING COMPARED TO THE FATE WE JUST DODGED!
NO...TRUE.
OH, LOOK, OUR HERO'S BACK!
?
NIGHT IS NIGH AND THE COLD WITH IT. WHY HAVEN'T YOU MADE A FIRE?
'CAUSE LIGHTING A FIRE WITH NO MATCHES IS LIKE GETTING A COW'S EYES TO LIGHT UP WITH CURIOSITY. IT DOESN'T HAPPEN!

BY THE BLOOD OF THE FROZEN! USE THAT TONE WITH ME AGAIN, YOUNG LADY, AND YOU'LL GET A HIDING!
MMPFFF !!
AND YOU! INSTEAD OF SNICKERING LIKE A FOOL, GO FETCH SOME WOOD! NOT KINDLING.
I SAID THE COLD WOULD COME SOON. THIS IS NO PICNIC OUTING.
?
FFSSSSHHH
!

!
FOOOSH
HERE YA GO, BOSS! WOULD'VE FELLED A TREE FOR YA, BUT--?!
WHOA! THAT'S SOME BLAZE! HOW'D YOU GET IT GOING?
SIT DOWN, YOUNG LADY. YOU'VE GOT SOME EXPLAINING TO DO.
I WANT TO HEAR IT ALL, FROM THE BEGINNING.

THAT NIGHT...
GOING FROM YOUR WORLD TO GWENDALAVIR MUST HAVE BEEN QUITE A SURPRISE.
ALTHOUGH WE HAVE LONG KNOWN THAT OUR TWO WORLDS EXIST SIDE BY SIDE, AND IT IS POSSIBLE TO PASS BACK AND FORTH...
...TRUE IMAGINATORS WHO CAN DO SO ARE FEW AND FAR BETWEEN.
IMAGINATORS?
THOSE WHO CAN MAKE WHAT THEY MERELY IMAGINE INTO A REALITY. THEIR MINDS PASS INTO THE DIMENSION WE CALL THE IMAGINARIUM, AND MAKE THEIR WAY ALONG SPIRAL PATHS KNOWN AS...
...THE GYRES.
THE MORE POWERFUL AN IMAGINATOR, THE FARTHER ALONG THE GYRES HE CAN TRAVEL, AND THE MORE HE CAN ALTER REALITY.
THE MOST TALENTED CAN IMAGINE THEMSELVES ELSEWHERE AND, BY DOING SO, TRANS-PORT THEMSELVES THERE AT ONCE.
THIS STEP IS KNOWN AS SIDESTRIDING. AND THE STEP THAT ALLOWS YOU TO PASS FROM YOUR WORLD TO MINE IS KNOWN AS THE GREAT STRIDE.

THAT STONE YOU FOUND IS LIKELY A GRAPHISPHERE -- AN ITEM OF INESTIMABLE AID TO IMAGINATORS.
THE CREATURE YOU TOOK IT FROM, CAMILLE, IS A TS'LIK, A FEARSOME MONSTER WELL-VERSED NOT ONLY IN IMAGINATING, BUT IN BATTLE AS WELL.
FORTUNATELY, TS'LIKS CANNOT PASS BETWEEN WORLDS. THEY CAN ONLY STRIDE BETWEEN LOCATIONS WITHIN A SINGLE WORLD.
DOUBTLESS, THE TS'LIK SET THOSE WALKERS ON YOUR HEELS TO RECOVER ITS PROPERTY.
NOT VERY REASSURING...
AND THOSE SPIDERS? THE WALKERS?
THE TS'LIKS TRAIN WALKERS TO KILL FOR THEM REMOTELY, SINCE THEY CANNOT MAKE THE GREAT STRIDE.
RIIIGHT. SO WHAT'S ALL THIS GOT TO DO WITH CAMILLE?
I KNOW NOT, MY GOOD MAN. OURS IS A DARK AGE.

HUMANS MAY HAVE FOUNDED THE EMPIRE OF GWENDALAVIR, BUT TODAY, IT IS GRAVELY THREATENED.
CAREFUL. IT'S QUITE STRONG.
FOR GENERATIONS, WE HAVE STAVED OFF INVASIONS OF THE RAIE, A NON-HUMAN SPECIES FROM THE NORTH.
SADLY, THE TS'LIKS, WHO CONTROL THE RAIES, HAVE MANAGED TO SEAL OFF ACCESS TO THE GYRES.
ALAVIRIAN IMAGINATORS MUST NOW MAKE DO WITH SIMPLE IMAGININGS... BEGINNER'S SKETCHES, YOU MIGHT SAY.
KOF KOFF! WHOO-EE! YOU WEREN'T KIDDING! THIS IS GOOD STUFF!
NOW, AS I SAID, THE GREAT STRIDE IS AN EXTREMELY POWERFUL ACT. THAT YOU MANAGED TO PERFORM IT IS ASTONISHING.
YOUR COMING MUST BE A SIGN OF THE GREATEST IMPORT!

GYRES, SKETCHES... I NEED TO KNOW MORE, EDWIN. AM I AN IMAGINATOR?
I AM CONVINCED OF IT. ENOUGH TO ABANDON THE QUEST THAT LED ME HERE. MOREOVER, I REGRET HAVING COME ON FOOT. WE SHALL SORELY MISS MY HORSE TOMORROW.
LIGHTING A FIRE IS SOMETHING MANY HERE KNOW HOW TO DO. BUT YOU USED COLORS THAT THE TS'LIKS KEEP US FROM ACCESSING, AS IF THEIR SEAL HAS NO EFFECT ON YOU.
BUT BEWARE!
TOO CUNNING AN IMAGINATING MAY ATTRACT THE ATTENTION OF HOSTILE CREATURES. FROM NOW ON, YOU MUST BE CAREFUL. DO YOU UNDERSTAND?
YES, I UNDERSTAND.
CAN'T YOU SEND US BACK HOME?
SUCH IMAGINATING IS BEYOND ME, AND I HAVE NEVER ATTEMPTED THE GREAT STRIDE.
I FEAR YOU MUST FEND FOR YOURSELVES.
DO YOU KNOW ANYONE WHO COULD HELP US?

NO.
TIME TO SLEEP. TOMORROW WILL BE HARD.
DOESN'T MATTER MUCH IF I'M HERE, OR AT THE TOWERS. IT'S NOT LIKE ANYONE WILL NOTICE I'M GONE.
BUT YOU MIGHT GET IN TROUBLE, HUH, CAMILLE?
DEFINITELY, ONCE I'M BACK. BUT SINCE I CAN'T DO ANYTHING ABOUT IT, I'M NOT GOING TO WORRY TOO MUCH FOR NOW.
A WISE CHOICE, GIRL.
SLEEP?
MM-HMM...
THE IMAGINARIUM, GYRES, THE GREAT STRIDE... TS'LIKS!
?
EWILAN

GET UP. WE'VE A LONG WAYS TO GO.
WHERE TO?
BEYOND THE GREAT FOREST OF BARAIL THAT DIVIDES THE WESTLANDS OF THE EMPIRE FROM FAEL COUNTRY.
THAT IS WHERE I WAS BOUND BEFORE I MET YOU -- IN HOPES OF FORGING AN ALLIANCE WITH THE FAELS. WE'RE CAUGHT BETWEEN THE RAIE INVASION FROM THE NORTH...
...AND THE ALINE PIRATES PLUNDERING TO THE SOUTH.
SOUNDS LIKE SOME HEAVY STUFF.
IF WE DO NOTHING, THE EMPIRE WILL CRUMBLE.
MEANWHILE, LET'S GIVE IT OUR BEST.

DID YOU NEVER WALK MUCH IN YOUR WORLD?
WE RIDE IN CARS, TRAINS, AND PLANES. THEY'RE FASTER AND NOT AS TIRING.
I SEE.
DOES OUR WORLD BORE YOU?
I'VE READ THE ACCOUNTS OF TRAVELERS WHO'VE BEEN THERE AND BACK, BUT TO BE HONEST, I'VE NEVER BEEN INTERESTED.
I HAVE ENOUGH WORK AND SURPRISES HERE TO KEEP ME BUSY.
TIME TO MOVE ON.
IF ALL GOES WELL, TONIGHT WE SLEEP IN REAL BEDS.
IN THE EMPIRE'S CAPITAL?
AL-JEIT IS HUNDREDS OF MILES AWAY. I SPEAK OF THE INN AT AL-VOR, THE LARGEST CITY IN THE REGION.

WHEN I GET BACK, MY PARENTS ARE GOING TO HACK ME UP INTO TINY PIECES! IN THE MEANTIME, I FEEL LIKE I'M HAVING THE BEST DREAM EVER! RIGHT, SALIM?
YOU SAID IT, GIRL!
BEHIND ME! QUICK!
?
YOU MUST HAVE LEFT A PIECE OF YOURSELF TRAILING BEHIND IN THE IMAGINARIUM. IT DREW THEM HERE!
?
WHAT THE--?!
WHAT THE HECK IS THAT?
GET OUT OF THE GYRES! DO IT! NOW!
DO YOU KNOW ME, TS'LIK?
ALL TS'LIKS KNOW OF EDWIN TILL'ILLAN.
THEN WHY DID YOUR STRIDING BRING YOU HERE?
I SEEK THAT WHICH IS MINE.

THE GRAPHI-SPHERE?
I CARE NOT FOR THE GRAPHISPHERE! IT IS EWILAN I SEEK. IT IS SHE I HAVE COME TO TAKE, IN ORDER TO PUT AN END TO THIS STORY!
EWILAN...?!
DON'T TELL ME THAT YOU -- THE EMPIRE'S OWN GUARD DOG -- DIDN'T KNOW WHOM YOU WERE ESCORTING!
BUT IT MATTERS NOT! SHE IS MINE!
YOU CLAIMED TO KNOW ME. THEN YOU KNOW IF YOU DEFY ME, YOUR KIND WILL LOSE ONE OF ITS OWN?
I KNOW, EDWIN TILL'ILLAN.
THE LEGENDS SPEAK OF YOU AS THE WARRIOR WHO FOUR TIMES OVER SUCCEEDED IN DEFEATING TS'LIK WARRIORS. BUT NOT EVEN ONE SO FORMIDABLE CAN SURVIVE A CLASH WITH TWO OF US AT ONCE!

WELL, EDWIN TILL'ILLAN?
WILL YOU GRANT ME THAT WHICH I CAME TO SEEK, OR WILL YOU TRY TO ADD ANOTHER FEAT TO YOUR LEGEND?
CAMILLE, GRAB THE THREE RODS FROM MY BAG AND STICK THEM IN THE GROUND BEHIND ME.
THEY ARE MERWYN'S CLARIONS. NO MATTER THE OUTCOME OF THIS BATTLE, THEY'LL AFFORD YOU TEN MINUTES' HEAD START.
BUT--
YOU HAVEN'T SEEN THE LAST OF ME. I'LL DO MY BEST TO CATCH UP.
CAMILLE, DO NO IMAGINATING! STAY AS FAR AWAY FROM THE GYRES AS YOU CAN, OR THEY'LL FIND YOU.
NOW, RUN!
RUN!!

DON'T YOU THINK WE SHOULD CHECK AND SEE WHAT HAPPENED TO HIM?
NO. HE SAID HE'D CATCH UP. AND IF THE TS'LIKS BEAT HIM, LET'S NOT MAKE THEIR JOB ANY EASIER BY GOING BACK.
SO...WHY DID THOSE INSECTOIDS CALL YOU EWILAN, AND WHAT'S THIS LEGEND ALL ABOUT?
I'M WONDERING THE SAME THING, SALIM. I HAVE NO IDEA.
SO PLEASE QUIT BADGERING ME WITH QUESTIONS AND KEEP WALKING!
BADGERING? BUT --
EDWIN TOLD US TO HEAD EAST FOR AL-VOR. EAST MUST BE THAT WAY. WHAT DO YOU THINK?
IF YOU HEAD NORTHEAST, YOU'LL REACH A TRAIL THAT WILL LEAD YOU STRAIGHT TO AL-VOR.
HOW DO YOU KNOW?
SALIM? CAN YOU HEAR ME?
WHO SAID THAT? WHERE ARE YOU?
THERE'S NOTHING TO BE SEEN.
YOUR FRIEND ISN'T HERE AT PRESENT. HE'S IN NO DANGER. NOW WE CAN TALK IN PRIVATE.

I DON'T WANT TO TALK TO YOU!
RELEASE SALIM AND TAKE A LONG WALK OFF A SHORT PIER, GOT IT?
YOU REALLY DO HAVE QUITE A TEMPER! STOP SHOUTING. I CAN HEAR YOU JUST FINE.
WHERE ARE YOU? NO, FIRST OFF, WHO ARE YOU?
I AM FAR AWAY FROM HERE, IN AL-POLL.
I AM ELEA RIL'MORIENVAL, A SENTINEL.
A...SENTINEL?
WE SENTINELS ONCE KEPT THE EMPIRE SAFE. UNTIL THE TS'LIKS LOCKED US AWAY AND SET A GUARD UPON US.
NOW WE ARE KNOWN AS THE FROZEN ONES. WE CAN NO LONGER MOVE, AND OUR POWERS ARE PARALYZED.
DO YOU KNOW WHY I'M HERE?
OF COURSE. IT WAS I WHO BROUGHT YOU HERE.
YOU WERE BORN HERE, IN THE WORLD YOU SEE BEFORE YOU. I KNEW YOUR PARENTS.
MY PARENTS!
WH-WHAT ELSE DO YOU KNOW?

I HAVEN'T TIME TO EXPLAIN EVERYTHING IN DETAIL. YOU MUST GET TO AL-VOR AS FAST AS YOU CAN AND FIND MASTER ANALYST DUOM NIL'ERG. HE WILL TEST YOU AND FIND OUT WHY YOU ENDED UP HERE, INSTEAD OF YOUR BROTHER.
MY BROTHER?
GO SEE DUOM. HE WILL GUIDE YOU. OUR ONLY HOPE IS THAT YOU HAVE ENOUGH OF A GIFT TO BRING US YOUR BROTHER. HE ALONE HAS THE POWER TO FREE US ALL.
I'VE USED ALL MY ENERGY IN REACHING OUT TO YOU. I SHALL BE POWERLESS NOW FOR A LONG WHILE TO COME -- PERHAPS YEARS.
WAIT! I DON'T KNOW HOW I GOT HERE, OR HOW TO LEAVE. AND I NEVER KNEW I HAD A BROTHER TILL NOW!
YOU ARE NOT AS HELPLESS AS YOU THINK. YOU ARE THE DAUGHTER OF ELICIA AND ALTAN GIL'SAYAN.
REMEMBER: YOUR BROTHER, AL-POLL. OUR WORLD IS COUNTING ON YOU, EWILAN.
STARING AT BIRDS NOW, ARE WE? WE'D BETTER FIGURE OUT OUR NEXT MOVE,
YOU'RE RIGHT. WE'LL HEAD NORTHEAST AND PICK UP THE ROAD TO AL-VOR.
I'VE GOT ONE HECK OF A STORY FOR THE ROAD. YOU READY?
WHEN YOU ARE!

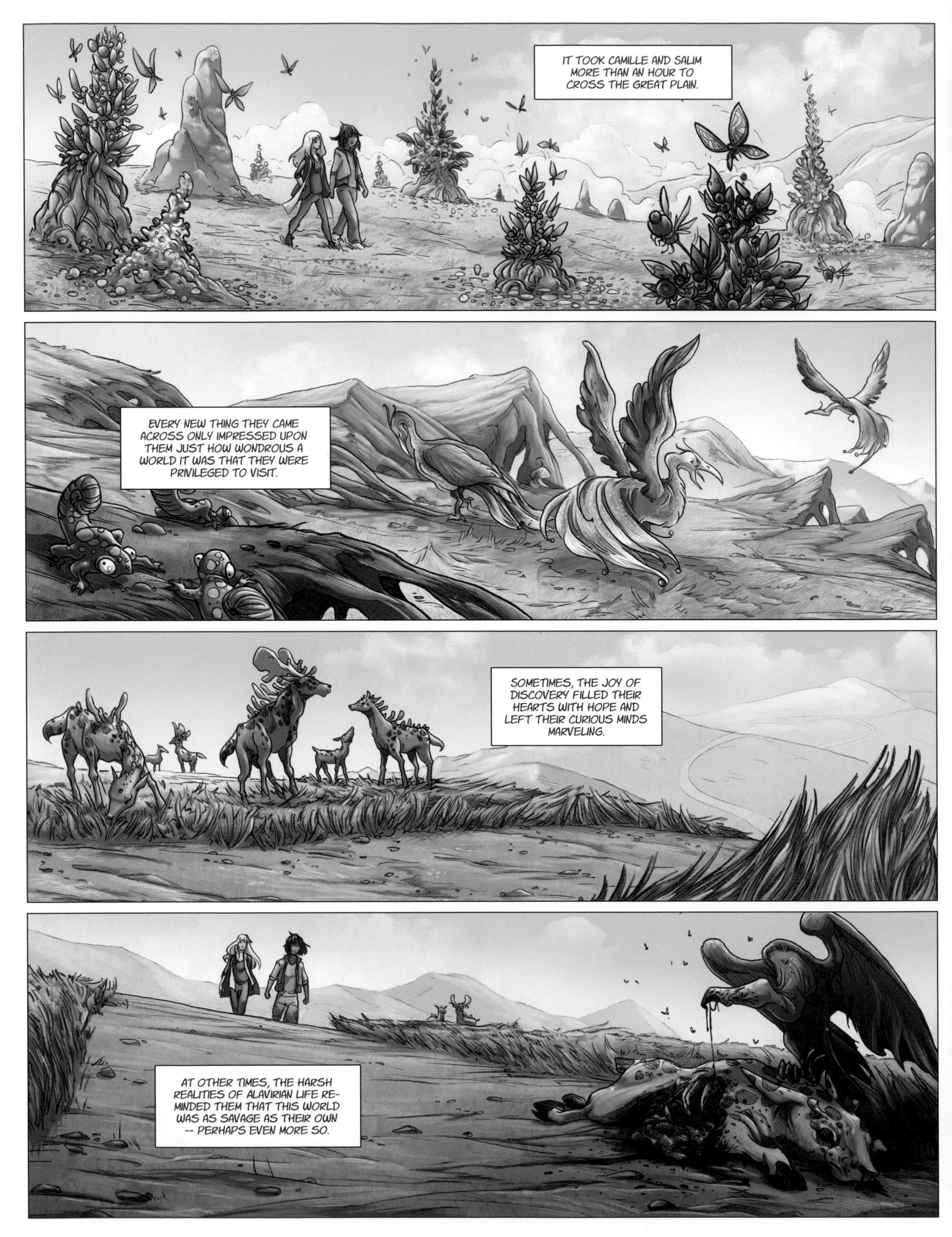
IT TOOK CAMILLE AND SALIM MORE THAN AN HOUR TO CROSS THE GREAT PLAIN.
EVERY NEW THING THEY CAME ACROSS ONLY IMPRESSED UPON THEM JUST HOW WONDROUS A WORLD IT WAS THAT THEY WERE PRIVILEGED TO VISIT.
SOMETIMES, THE JOY OF DISCOVERY FILLED THEIR HEARTS WITH HOPE AND LEFT THEIR CURIOUS MINDS MARVELING.
AT OTHER TIMES, THE HARSH REALITIES OF ALAVIRIAN LIFE RE-MINDED THEM THAT THIS WORLD WAS AS SAVAGE AS THEIR OWN -- PERHAPS EVEN MORE SO.

AT LONG LAST, THEY FOUND THE ROAD ELEA RIL'MORIENVAL HAD MENTIONED. PERHAPS IT WAS TIME FOR A BRIEF RESPITE?
BUT WHEN THEY BEHELD THE CITY OF AL-VOR...
...THEY KNEW THAT THEY HAD NOT YET EARNED THEIR REST.
WELL? WHAT DO YOU THINK, GIRL?
THEY REALIZED THAT THEIR ADVENTURE HAD ONLY JUST BEGUN.

CAMILLE, DID YOU SEE THAT THING?
DREAM ON, SALIM. WE CAN'T BUY ANYTHING HERE!
NEED I REMIND YOU THAT WE'RE NOT HERE TO GAPE AND GAWK, BUT TO FIND AN ANALYST NAMED DUOM!
SO HOW DO YOU PLAN ON FINDING THIS GUY? YOU'VE SEEN THE SIZE OF THIS CITY.
YOU'RE RIGHT. IT'S LIKE WE'RE BACK IN MEDIEVAL TIMES.
IT'S CRAZY! EVERYTHING'S MADE OF STONE! NOT A BLOCK OF CONCRETE OR A SINGLE ELECTRICAL WIRE -- NOT EVEN A SATELLITE DISH!
SHH! WE DON'T WANT TO BE TOO CONSPICUOUS.

SAY, ARE WE GOING IN CIRCLES? WE'VE BEEN IN THIS STREET BEFORE.
FOR SOME REASON I PICTURED THIS DUOM AS HAVING A SHOP, BUT I HAVE NO IDEA WHY
WHY DON'T WE JUST ASK SOMEONE?
SURE, BUT WHO? WE DON'T KNOW ANYTHING ABOUT HIM BESIDES HIS NAME. "ANALYST" MIGHT NOT EVEN BE A TRADE.
HOW ABOUT THERE?
THE SLEEPING DOG
THE SLEEPING DOG
YOU CAN BE REAL CLEVER WHEN YOU TRY!
...AND JUST AS THE TS'LIK WAS ABOUT TO DELIVER THE KILLING BLOW --
-- I MANAGED TO FREE MY AXE AT LAST.
YEAH? AND WHERE'D YOU STUFF THE BODY, YOU BIG OAF?
I WAS JUST ABLE TO PARRY THE BLOW, AND WITH A SINGLE SWIFT BACKHAND STROKE, LOPPED OFF ITS HIDEOUS HEAD.
AW, IT WAS ... WASN'T IT?

DON'T BELIEVE ME? JUST YOU WAIT!
LOOK, EVERYONE! I'VE GOT THE PROOF RIGHT HERE!
LET HER GO, JACKASS!
OW! YOU'RE HURTING ME!
WHAT WERE YOU, BORN WITH COW DUNG FOR BRAINS? YOU DON'T JUST GRAB PEOPLE BY THE ARM LIKE THAT!
MY APOLOGIES, LASS.
BUT YOU WERE THERE WHEN I BATTLED THE TS'LIK. I THOUGHT YOU MIGHT CORROBORATE MY ACCOUNT.
THAT KNIGHT IN ARMOR -- THAT WAS YOU?
WHY, YES! MIGHT YOU CONFIRM THAT I INDEED SLEW THAT MONSTER?
I DID INDEED SEE THIS KNIGHT VALIANTLY CONFRONT A TS'LIK.
DRINKS ALL 'ROUND! TOAST THE KNIGHT'S HEALTH! HIC!
THANKS TO YOU, LASS, MY HONOR IS INTACT. I AM IN YOUR DEBT.

A FEW TANKARDS LATER...
BURP! EXCUSE ME.
WE REALLY SHOULD BE GOING, BJORN. WE'VE GOT A LONG QUEST AHEAD OF US.
?
WHY DIDN'T YOU SAY SO EARLIER? BJORN WAL'WAYARD IS YOUR MAN! WHAT'S IT ALL ABOUT?
IT'S NOT A MATTER OF FIGHT-ING, BJORN.
THAT MATTERS NOT! HOW MAY I BE OF SERVICE?
WE SEEK A MAN NAMED DUOM NIL'ERG.
THE ANALYST! WHAT BUSINESS HAVE YOU WITH HIM, PRAY TELL?
HOW SILLY OF ME! QUESTS ARE PRIVATE AFFAIRS. SAY NO MORE. I SHALL TAKE YOU TO HIM.
CARRY ON WITH THE FESTIVITIES! I SHALL RETURN FORTHWITH.
DUTY CALLS!

DUOM NIL'ERG ANALYST
TA-DAA!
HERE WE PART WAYS. I WOULD RATHER FACE A SAVANNAH TIGER BAREHANDED THAN DUOM NIL'ERG.
I'LL LIKELY TARRY A FEW DAYS YET AT THE SLEEPING DOG. SHOULD YOU NEED ME, YOU KNOW WHERE TO LOOK!
GOTCHA, BJORN! THANKS!
LADIES FIRST!
WHAT IS IT?
I'M LOOKING FOR DUOM NIL'ERG -- TO BE TESTED.
DON'T WASTE MY TIME. YOU'RE FAR TOO YOUNG FOR TESTING.
AND MY RATES ARE FAR BEYOND YOUR WILD-EST IMAGININGS.
I'LL PAY THEM, AND THEN SOME!
OH, REALLY? WHAT WITH?

THIS!
A GRAPHI-SPHERE!
HOW DID YOU COME TO POSSESS IT?
OH, I JUST FOUND IT ON THE GROUND. WILL YOU ACCEPT IT AS PAYMENT?
THIS SPHERE IS OF TS'LIK MAKE. IT IS PRICELESS, BUT NO HUMAN CAN USE IT.
BUT YOU MUST TEST ME!
TUT TUT, YOUNG LADY. I SHALL ANALYZE YOU -- FOR FREE, SINCE YOU INSIST.
THIS WAY.
THANK YOU VERY MUCH FOR YOUR TIME.
OH, DON'T THANK ME.
I DOUBT I'LL OBTAIN ANY CONCLUSIVE RESULTS! A TRUE GIFT IS RARE INDEED.

THE COMBINATION OF THREE FORCES MAKE IMAGINATING POSSIBLE: WILL, POWER, AND CREATIVITY.
THESE FORCES MAY BE FOUND INSIDE EACH OF US. THE ANALYST'S TASK IS TO GAUGE THEIR INTENSITY.
RED IS FOR WILL.
YELLOW FOR POWER.
AND LASTLY, BLUE FOR CREATIVITY.
THESE WERE THE RESULTS OF OUR EMPEROR SIL'AFIAN. AS YOU CAN SEE, HIS WILL IS NEARLY INHUMAN, AND HIS POWER SIZEABLE, BUT HIS LACK OF CREATIVITY KEEPS HIM FROM BEING A TRUE IMAGINATOR.
THAT SAID, NO ONE'S ASKING HIM TO IMAGINATE, BUT RATHER TO GOVERN. AND TO THAT END, HIS RESULTS ARE IDEAL.
UH...YOU GET ANY OF THAT, CAMILLE?
SURE! DIDN'T YOU?

NO, BUT I ZONED OUT A BIT. HOW'S IT GONNA HELP YOU KNOWING HOW BIG YOUR CIRCLES ARE?
KNOWING THE NATURE OF MY POWER WILL HELP ME WIELD IT, DUMMY!
SIT DOWN, YOUNG LADY.
THE SCINTILLATOR IS A HIGHLY SENSITIVE DEVICE. IT EXTENDS INTO THE IMAGINARIUM. IF YOU ARE ABLE TO IMAGINATE, IT WILL KNOW.
READY?
YES.
WHAT SHOULD I DO?
NOTHING. LET THE SCINTILLATOR GUIDE YOU. I SHALL GUIDE THE SCINTILLATOR.

?!
IT CAN'T BE!
I HAVE ONLY SEEN SUCH A RESULT IN BOOKS!
WHO...
JUST WHO ARE YOU?!

SO YOU ARE EWILAN GIL'SAYAN.
I SHOULD HAVE GUESSED.
YOU LOOK JUST LIKE YOUR MOTHER, AND YOUR RESULTS CONFIRM THAT YOU ARE A HIGHLY GIFTED IMAGINATOR.
PUT THESE CLOTHES ON. THEY WILL BE MUCH MORE PRACTICAL FOR THE JOURNEY WE ARE ABOUT TO MAKE.
YOUR BLACK CIRCLE INDICATES THAT YOU ARE THE PERFECT IMAGINATOR, EWILAN.
IT ALSO EXPLAINS WHY YOU CAN USE THE TS'LIK GRAPHISPHERE AND HAVE MADE THE GREAT STRIDE MORE THAN ONCE!
BUT THE TS'LIKS KNOW YOU'VE RETURNED. THEY'LL DO ANYTHING THEY CAN TO ELIMINATE YOU.
WE MUST REACH THE EMPIRE'S CAPITAL, AL-JEIT, AS SOON AS WE CAN. ONLY THERE WILL YOU BE SAFE.
BUT WHAT ABOUT ELEA? MY PARENTS?
THEY WERE MEMBERS OF AN ORDER OF THE EMPIRE'S ELITE IMAGINATORS.
?
LOOK...

TWELVE IN NUMBER, THE SENTINELS WERE THE MOST POWERFUL IMAGINATORS. THEIR DUTY: TO WATCH THE MANY GYRES WINDING THROUGH THE IMAGINARIUM. THEY KEPT THE TS'LIK THREAT CONTAINED AND GWENDALAVIR KNEW PEACE FOR ALMOST FIFTEEN CENTURIES.
BUT JUST OVER SEVEN YEARS AGO, ONE AMONG THEM, ELEA RIL'MORIENVAL, LED SEVEN OF THE OTHERS IN A REBELLION.
THEY WISHED TO DESERT THEIR POSTS, CLAIMING THAT THE TS'LIKS HAD LONG SINCE VANISHED.
IT IS SAID THEY WEARIED OF THEIR DIFFICULT TASK, AND WISHED TO ENJOY LIFE AND ITS PLEASURES.
ONLY YOUR PARENTS ROSE UP AGAINST WHAT THEY SAW AS TREASON. FOR THEM, THE TS'LIK THREAT WAS STILL QUITE REAL.
A VIOLENT CONFRONTATION ENSUED. YOUR PARENTS HAD TO FACE SEVEN OF THEIR FELLOWS ALONE. THE STRUGGLE WAS AN EPIC ONE: EVERY IMAGINATOR USING THEIR POWERS TO THE FULLEST.
DESPITE THEIR UTTER MASTERY OF IMAGINATING, YOUR PARENTS WERE DEFEATED.

TO EVERYONE'S MIS-
FORTUNE, NO MORE
WATCH WAS KEPT
OVER THE GYRES.

THE TS'LIKS SEIZED UPON YOUR PARENTS' DEFEAT AND ATTACKED. LONG BELIEVED VANISHED, THEY HAD ACTUALLY BEEN LYING IN WAIT ALL THE WHILE, HATCHING DARK PLANS FOR CONQUEST.

THE RENEGADE SENTINELS, WEAKENED BY THEIR RECENT CLASH WITH YOUR PARENTS, SOON FELL PREY TO THE TS'LIK ASSAULT.

THEY WERE STRIPPED OF THEIR POWERS, IMMOBILIZED, AND SHUT AWAY IN AN UNKNOWN PLACE. FROM THAT MOMENT ON, THEY WERE KNOWN AS THE FROZEN ONES.

WE HAVE LOOKED FOR THEM FAR AND WIDE, BUT ALWAYS IN VAIN. THANKS TO YOU, WE NOW KNOW THEY ARE BEING HELD CAPTIVE IN AL-POLL, A FORGOTTEN CITY OF THE NORTHERN MOUNTAINS.

WHAT ABOUT ELEA RIL'MORIENVAL? IS SHE BEHIND THE TS'LIK RESURGENCE?

WE DO NOT KNOW. I'M CONVINCED SHE HAD OTHER GOALS IN MIND. SHE LIKELY WISHED TO USE THE TS'LIKS TO SEIZE POWER, BUT THEY BETRAYED

AND SHE DARED REACH OUT TO ME TO ASK ME TO RESCUE HER? THAT SNAKE!
DO NOT JUDGE HER TOO RASHLY. SHE IS STILL A SENTINEL.
IT'S TIME. WE MUST LEAVE BEFORE THE TS'LIK SPIES SPOT YOU.
IT MIGHT BE TOO LATE FOR THAT, OLD MAN!
THE TS'LIKS ALREADY HAVE MERCENARIES ON YOUR TRAIL.
EDWIN!
I TOLD YOU I'D FIND YOU.
GET READY. WE LEAVE IMMEDIATELY.
THE JOURNEY WILL BE FRAUGHT WITH PERIL. DUOM, DO YOU KNOW ANY MEN WHO MIGHT LEND A HAND?
THERE'S THE CITY GUARD, BUT I FEAR THEY'VE GOT THEIR HANDS FULL ALREADY.
IF IT'S A BRAVE KNIGHT YOU'RE AFTER, I THINK I KNOW JUST THE MAN!

TRAVELING BY NIGHT PROVED RESTFUL, BUT AT DAYBREAK, THE LIGHT -- USUALLY SO WELCOME -- SEEMED TO EXPOSE EWILAN AND HER FRIENDS TO NEW DANGERS.
WELL, MY LADY? DOTH SLEEP EVADE YOU?
?
I EVADED SLEEP, IS MORE LIKE IT. ANY WORD FROM EDWIN?
NOT YET. HE LED A SCOUTING PARTY UP AHEAD.
I DON'T KNOW HOW HE'S STILL AWAKE AFTER FIGHTING OFF TWO TS'LIKS AND KEEPING WATCH ALL NIGHT. THAT MAN'S MADE OF STEEL!
HA HA HA! WHY DON'T YOU ASK HIM YOURSELF, BJORN? HERE HE COMES!
WE'VE BEEN SPOTTED. FIVE HUNDRED YARDS AWAY, TWENTY-SOME ARMED MEN ARE WAITING TO AMBUSH US!

THEY'RE MOUNTED. THEY'LL BE MOVING FASTER THAN US. PREPARE FOR A FIGHT!
BJORN, STAY WITH THE WAGON AND PROTECT CAMILLE. WITH YOUR LIFE!
FEAR NOT, MY LADY. I'VE ALREADY FOUGHT OFF A TS'LIK FOR YOU. A FEW BANDITS DON'T FRIGHTEN ME!
AND ME?
STAY WITH CAMILLE. I'LL RIDE AHEAD WITH HANS AND MANIEL. FOLLOW CLOSE.
WE'LL TRY TO FORCE OUR WAY THROUGH. IF THEY SWARM US, HOLD YOUR GROUND AND WE'LL FALL BACK AROUND YOU.
YOOU OKAY?
I'VE SEEN WORSE, YOUNG MAN. WITH EDWIN ON OUR SIDE, WE HAVE A GOOD CHANCE OF PULLING THROUGH. GIDDYAP!

NO MATTER WHAT HAPPENS, YOU TWO STAY IN THE WAGON. UNDER-STOOD?
GOT IT, BOSS!
BJORN! WATCH OUT!
??

HE--?!
YES, SALIM! DUOM'S IMAGI-NATING!
BUT THE TS'LIK SEAL KEEPS HIM FROM BRINGING IT TO LIFE!
?

BJORN! EDWIN'S COMING BACK WITH YOUR FRIENDS.
HANS! MANIEL! FLANK THEM!
BJORN, CAMILLE'S ALL YOURS!
KNOW WHAT, GIRL? IF WE DON'T MAKE IT, I WANTED TO SAY THAT -- ?!

BY THE BLOOD OF THE FROZEN!
WELL, THEY'LL LEAVE US ALONE FOR A BIT. WE MUST BE OFF AS QUICK AS WE CAN.
SHOULD WE NOT BURY THE DEAD?
GO AHEAD, IF YOU'VE TIME TO WASTE. I'VE GOT A MISSION. I'M PRESSING ON.
SALIM, I...
CAMILLE!
CAMILLE...
WHAT HAPPENED? ARE YOU OKAY?

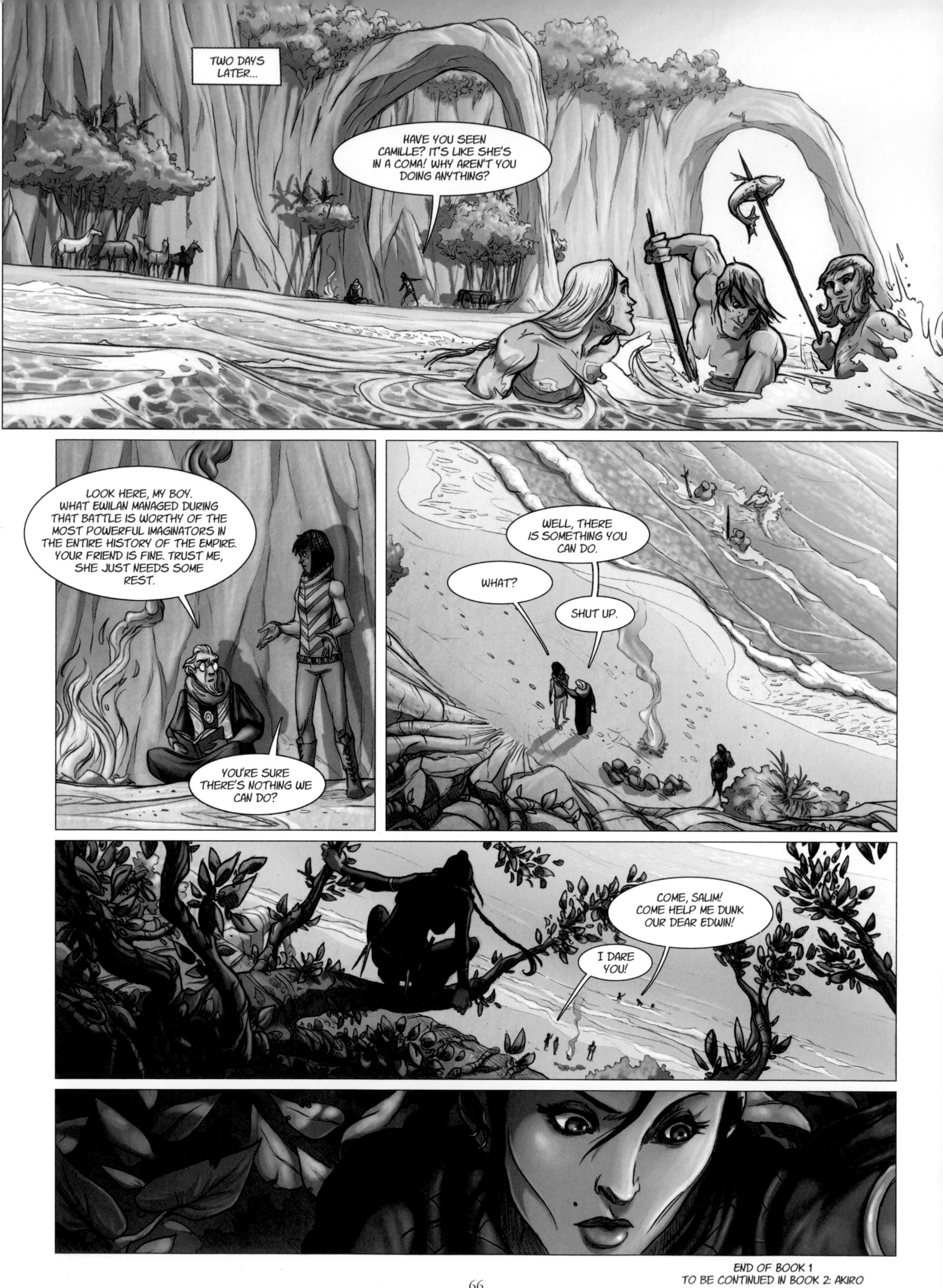

END OF BOOK 1
TO BE CONTINUED IN BOOK 2: AKIRO

OTHER BOOKS FROM EUROCOMICS/IDW

CORTO MALTESE BY HUGO PRATT

THE ADVENTURES OF DIETER LUMPEN
BY JORGE ZENTNER & RUBÉN PELLEJERO

THE SILENCE OF MALKA
BY JORGE ZENTNER & RUBÉN PELLEJERO

PARACUELLOS BY CARLOS GIMÉNEZ

FLIGHT OF THE RAVEN BY JEAN-PIERRE GIBRAT

THE REPRIEVE BY JEAN-PIERRE GIBRAT

ALACK SINNER BY CARLOS SAMPAYO & JOSÉ MUÑOZ

JEROME K. JEROME BLOCHE BY ALAIN DODIER

LIGHTS OF THE AMALOU
BY CHRISTOPHE GIBELIN & CLAIRE WENDLING

ONE MAN, ONE ADVENTURE:
THE MAN FROM THE GREAT NORTH
BY HUGO PRATT

TALES FROM THE AGE OF THE COBRA
BY ENRIQUE FERNÁNDEZ

VIOLETTE
BY TERESA RADICE & STEFANO TURCONI

FOUR SISTERS
BY MALIKA FERDJOUKH & CATI BAUR